The vacuum cleaner sitting in the middle of the living room means Christine cleaned the house. Therefore, no vacuum clearly means no cleaning.

This appears to be Christine's husband's logic.

So she'll always leave proof of the day's householding tasks in strategic spots, and harvest the praise for a job well done.

Most of the time, her husband's blind spot makes her seethe—except when it gives her the freedom she needs to take care of business.

R.W. WALLACE
Author of the Ghost Detective Series

OUT OF SIGHT
A Mystery Short Story

Out of Sight
by R.W. Wallace

Copyright © 2019 by R.W. Wallace

Cover by the author
Copy edit by Jinxie Gervasio
Cover Illustration 32041902 © Iriana Shiyan | 123rf.com

All characters and events in this book, other than those clearly in the public domain, are fictitious and any resemblance to real persons, living or dead, is purely coincidental.

All rights reserved. No part of this publication may be reproduced, distributed, or transmitted in any form or by any means, including photocopying, recording, or other electronic or mechanical methods, without the prior written permission of the publisher, except in the case of brief quotations embodied in critical reviews and certain other noncommercial uses permitted by copyright law. For permission requests, write to the publisher, addressed "Attention: Permissions Coordinator," at the address below.

www.rwwallace.com

ISBN: [979-10-95707-07-3]

Main category—Fiction
Other category—Mystery

First Edition

14 13 12 11 10 / 10 9 8 7 6 5 4 3 2 1

Also by R.W. Wallace

Mystery

The Tolosa Mystery Series
The Red Brick Haze (free)
The Red Brick Cellars
The Red Brick Basilica

Ghost Detective Shorts (coming soon)
Just Desserts
Lost Friends
Family Bonds
Till Death
Common Ground

Short Stories
Cold Blue Eternity
Hidden Horrors
Critters
Gertrude and the Trojan Horse
First Impressions
Let Them Eat Cake
Two's Company

Science Fiction (short stories)
The Vanguard
Quarantine (Lollapalooza)
Common Enemies (Lollapalooza)

Adventure (short stories)
Size Matters

Fantasy (short stories)
Morbier Impossible
A Second Chance
Unexpected Consequences

OUT OF SIGHT

Gérard Blanc walked through the door at five to seven, while Christine Blanc sat curled up in the corner of the couch, reading a mystery novel. She'd sat there for exactly twenty minutes, grabbing her daily dose of time for herself.

The house was tidy and clean, the fridge was full of groceries, her son had finished his homework and was currently drowning himself in music in his room, and the trash cans were already on the sidewalk, ready for tomorrow morning. She deserved some time-out with a funny detective and gritty murders.

Tomorrow she'd be back at work, with everyone asking her how her "second weekend" had been. Always said with a wink and a laugh, because everybody knew that the moms taking Wednesdays off didn't do it to slack off, but it hurt—just a little—nonetheless. Her son Louis might be fifteen, so he didn't exactly need her to take him to the park anymore—though she did drive him to soccer practice in the afternoon—but there was still a ton of stuff to do. And since she had this day off every week, everybody—with her husband Gérard first in line—assumed this meant all household tasks fell to her.

Need to go to the bank? Christine can do it on Wednesday. Louis needs new clothes? Christine can do it on Wednesday. Laundry? Cut the grass? Dentist's appointment for Louis? Wednesday.

She didn't mind doing the work. Really. She loved being useful to her family and enjoying a pretty home. There were just some…details…yet to be worked out for everything to run smoothly.

"Ah, you vacuumed, I see," Gérard said as he spotted the vacuum in the middle of the living room. "Excellent." He removed his leather shoes, placed them in the shoe rack by the door, deposited his bag in its usual spot in the closet, and approached his wife with a genuine smile.

He leaned over the back of the couch and gave her a kiss on the top of her head. "Did you have a good day?" His scruff caught in Christine's hair and she caught a faint whiff of his deodorant mixed with sweat. It had been a sweltering hot day. Apparently even the air-conditioning in the office wasn't enough when wearing a suit and tie.

Christine closed her book and returned her husband's smile. "Yes, thank you," she replied. "I'll just put away the vacuum, and dinner will be ready in five minutes. Would you mind telling Louis to come down?"

Gérard cocked his head in direction of their son's room as he removed his tie. "He's going to go deaf if he continues like that."

Christine shrugged.

"I guess he had to turn into a real teenager at some point." Gérard hung his jacket in the closet before taking the steps two at a time. "Louis! Dinner in five."

Christine had to force her frown away. Louis *had* changed in the last couple of months. He always listened to his music, didn't come down to talk to her when he'd finished his homework, hardly ever smiled.

Somehow, she'd thought she'd gotten the perfect boy. Who wouldn't rebel and stay her little darling.

The music blared even louder, meaning Gérard opened Louis's door. Christine winced. She wouldn't say anything.

It wouldn't help.

☙

As CHRISTINE WALKED through the front door, she was hit first by a blast of the welcome fresh air of a house where the stores had been closed all day, then by a deafening wall of angry music.

Closing the door behind her, Christine stood still in the hallway for several moments, staring at the stairwell leading to her son's room.

The house looked so quiet. Stores down, uncluttered tables. Everything still.

But that *noise*.

She didn't even know what type of music it was. Perhaps *Rage Against the Machine*? The name certainly fit. It most certainly was *not* the rock and old French ballads he used to listen to. How she missed Georges Brassens.

With a deep breath, Christine pushed aside the lingering stress from work, took off her shoes, and went up the stairs.

She knocked on his door and waited a few seconds even though there was no way he could hear her.

"Louis?" she yelled as she opened the door. "You have to turn the music down!"

The room was pitch black. Blinds down and curtains drawn. Even the digital alarm clock was absent. He must have unplugged it.

Head pounding because of the noise, Christine flicked on the light and made a beeline for the stereo. Guessing the music was actually coming from Louis's phone, she pulled the plug.

Blessed silence. And ringing ears.

She wanted to yell at him. For ruining his hearing. For bothering the neighbors.

She didn't.

"Louis?" she said, her voice soft. "What's going on?"

The comforter moved on the bed, Louis completely covered and curling into a ball. "Go away. I'm sleeping."

Christine stared at the comforter, not daring to go sit next to him. "Did you do your homework?"

"Go away."

Christine considered opening the stores but decided she didn't need to antagonize him even further. She looked around the room, at a loss.

On the desk in the corner, usually covered in books and homework, a large, hairy ball.

Christine sucked in a breath and recoiled. Then she recognized it.

"You cut your hair?" In two strides she was at the desk, delving her hand into locks of curly blond hair. Gérard's electric razor was still plugged into the socket next to the desk, its little green light blinking as it charged its long-dead battery.

This time she went to the bed. She sat down next to the bundle that was her son and pulled at the comforter.

He'd shorn almost all his hair off. There couldn't be more than a centimeter left, leaving his scalp visible for the first time since he was two.

Christine put her hand on her son's head, needing the physical confirmation that the golden locks were gone.

Louis pushed her off the bed and disappeared back under the comforter. "I said, go away!"

Christine picked herself off the floor. She smoothed down her skirt. "Dinner will be ready in twenty minutes." Her voice was shaking.

"Not hungry. Go away."

She stood there, looking around at her son's room, wondering where her little boy had gone.

"How was Automation class today?" He'd been so enthusiastic about that class at the beginning of the school year.

"GO AWAY!"

☙

Wednesday night, and Christine was once again enjoying her twenty minutes of mystery reading.

Louis hadn't said a word to her in over a week that wasn't some version of "Go away," but she'd managed to lower the volume of the music. She'd gone into his room one afternoon while he was hiding/sleeping under the covers and lowered the volume to something that wouldn't maim her son and wouldn't bother the neighbors. He hadn't touched the volume button since.

But the angry music continued.

Five minutes to seven, and Gérard walked through the front door. He looked around while he undid his shoelaces and put away his shoes. "What have you been up to today?"

Christine shrugged as she put her book away. "The usual." Laundry, dishes, cleaning the bathroom, picking up a package at the post office, weeding the flower garden, checking that the well was dry for the fifth year running, bringing Louis to soccer practice, paying a couple of bills, cleaning all the ground floor windows.

"Hmm," Gérard said and sat down in front of the computer. A news site was open thirty seconds later.

"Dinner will be ready in five minutes," Christine said.

༄

"Does he just not eat anymore?" Gérard put his dirty plate in the dishwasher before grabbing a yogurt from the fridge.

"I'll take a plate up to his room." Christine piled Louis's plate with spaghetti carbonara—Louis's favorite.

"You'll just encourage him to keep up his shenanigans. If he can't come down to eat with us, he can go hungry."

Christine took the food up to her son's room. "I'll just put this here," she said, loud enough to be heard over the music. "It'll do you good to eat something. Do you need anything else?"

"Go away," Louis said from the comforter.

He wasn't screaming it anymore—Christine took that for an improvement.

Back downstairs, Gérard had changed into his working-around-the-house clothes and was cleaning the living room windows.

"What are you doing?" Christine asked, voice impressively calm.

"What does it look like? I'm cleaning the windows. You can hardly see anything through them when the sun hits in the morning."

Christine closed her eyes for a moment and took a deep breath. "I know. That's why I cleaned them this afternoon. You're cleaning clean windows."

Gérard looked around the living room, apparently really seeing for the first time. "Oh. Well. Right. What about upstairs?"

Waving toward the stairs, Christine replied, "You can go clean the windows upstairs."

Should she have left the cleaning stuff out so that he'd see that she'd done it? Left the clean clothes folded on the bed? Placed Louis's soccer shoes in plain view?

If he didn't see proof, it didn't happen.

Christine attacked the dishes.

ೞ

A WEEK LATER, Christine allowed herself an afternoon with her friend Florence, getting a much-needed break. They were at their favorite *salon de thé*, enjoying the shade, a cup of tea, and a slice of raspberry and pistachio pie.

"I'm telling you," Christine said after taking a sip of her tea. "He still goes to school and soccer practice, but other than that, he hasn't left his room in two weeks."

Florence licked her spoon to make sure there wasn't the smallest little crumb left. "Have you asked him what the problem is?"

"Of course I have. He just tells me to go away." Christine sighed. "I guess we're just starting in on the dreaded teenage years."

"Nah hah." Florence pointed her spoon at Christine. Her expression was much more serious than usual during one of their rare girls-only outings. "That's not normal behavior for any teenager. For yours, it's downright worrying. You have to get him to talk to you." Her mouth lifted in a crooked smile. "Maybe he has girl problems." The smile grew. "Or boy problems!"

Christine chuckled. There was nothing her friend loved more than a juicy piece of gossip—apparently even when the subject matter was her best friend's son.

"I really don't think that's it," she said.

Florence pointed her spoon again. "Then figure out what it is. Now." She leaned forward in her chair and lowered her voice. "Did you hear about Elisabeth's son?"

"Mathieu? He was in Louis's class. What about him?"

"Well." Florence raised her eyebrows, indicating today's gossip was about to be delivered. "Apparently, she's still raising hell with the school even after moving Mathieu to that private school on the other side of town."

Christine took another sip of her tea. It was a bit warm to be drinking tea, but tradition was tradition and her Lapsang Suchong with pie was sacred. "Is it still about that Automation teacher?"

"Yes. She's making all kinds of accusations, none of which are making any kind of sense. I mean, there are twenty-five kids in that class. And they all love the teacher—except for Elisabeth's kid." Florence picked up her spoon to fish up one last crumb and closed her eyes in bliss as she ate it. "If you ask me, I think the kid didn't get the class, and made up a story to get his mom to pull him out. Then she got carried away, and now everything's snowballing."

"Louis certainly never has anything but praise for the man," Christine agreed. "By the way, did you hear that Dorian's mom—ah, I never remember her name, it's something really short—has quit her job?"

"Oh!" Florence's eyes lit with glee. "I did hear. But my sources have it she was fired. She's just saying she quit to save face."

Chuckling, Christine leaned back in her chair. "Do tell."

૱

That night—after she'd had dinner with Gérard, after bringing a plate of food to Louis's room, after the dishes—Christine decided to follow her friend's advice. She knocked on Louis's door, waited five seconds, then entered.

He'd eaten some of the food. All the pasta was gone, and a little more than half of his steak was cooling on the plate by the door.

Christine moved the plate next to the staircase, then went back to her son's room and closed the door behind her, plunging them into complete darkness.

"So how was your day?" she asked as she carefully crossed the room, moving each foot slowly in front of the other, praying she wouldn't step on anything pointy. "Did you have fun at school?"

"Go away."

"How are your friends? I haven't seen any of them around lately. Are you still hanging out?"

The sound of Gérard slamming a window shut somewhere in the house.

"Will you please talk to me, Louis? What's wrong?"

"Go away."

Christine lay down on the bed next to her son, snuggling up close to his back. "Sorry, kiddo. No can do. It's my house."

"It's my room."

"True." She put a hand on his back and started moving it in small circles, like he'd loved her to do when he was little. "How do you manage to breathe in there?"

A sigh. "Opening on the other side."

"Ah. That's one less thing for me to worry about, I guess."

Silence.

"You worry about me breathing under my comforter?"

"Of course I do. I'm your mother. Sometimes, when my mind starts playing tricks on me, I come check on you at night to make sure you're still breathing."

"That's creepy, *Maman*."

"Okay." Christine continued her caresses, and little by little, she pulled the comforter down so Louis's head was exposed. She ran her hand over his head, feeling like she was touching a soft cushion. "Your head's oddly soft when your hair's that short," she said. "Makes me want to lie here and run my hand over it all night."

Louis's voice was a whisper. "'kay."

Encouraged, Christine tried again. "How are things at school, Louis?"

A sound that might have been a sigh, might have been a sob. Or a mix of the two. "Not great."

"Is it your friends?"

"No."

"Classes? You know we won't be mad if you get bad grades, right?"

"Grades are fine."

Christine paused. Her heart beat faster in her chest and her breath shortened.

"Teachers?" she asked.

"Teacher."

ଔ

THE REASON SO many French moms took Wednesdays off was that there was no school on Wednesday afternoon. It meant they had the morning to take care of the house, the garden, rendez-vous, and shopping, then spent the afternoon either playing with their young kids or driving the not so young ones to various sports and activities.

Teachers also had Wednesday afternoons off.

"Monsieur Georges!" Christine called as she strode out from behind the bush she'd been hiding behind for ten minutes. She had a perfect view of the teachers' entrance to the school but needed to be alert so her target didn't get away before she caught up with him.

"How lucky that I ran into you here," she said with a big smile.

Monsieur Georges stopped in his tracks and turned to face Christine. "*Bonjour*, Madame," he said. "And you are?"

Christine shook his hand. "I'm Christine Blanc. Louis's mom? He's in your Automation class."

"Ah, yes, of course." His tone was civil, but Christine could feel his eyes on her as he talked. "To what do I owe this honor?"

Hand to heart, Christine's smile widened even further. "Oh, I just wanted to thank you for being such a good teacher to our kids. I've heard nothing but praise since the beginning of the school year."

The teacher relaxed, and a polite smile appeared on his handsome face. Christine thought he must be in his late thirties. His eyes were a sharp blue and his dark blond hair ruffled into a studied mess.

"I'm glad to hear that, Madame," he said. "Now—"

"At times," Christine continued, "I almost wished Louis hadn't chosen your subject, because it was all he could talk about at night. You'd think he had ten classes a week with you, not just two. Monsieur Georges did this. Monsieur Georges said that. I've never laughed so hard in a class before. He went on and on."

Monsieur Georges nodded. "If it means they learned something, I'm happy to—"

"Now there's only a short month left of the school year, and I still haven't had the opportunity to thank you properly." Christine took hold of the teacher's elbow and started guiding him down the sidewalk. "As luck would have it, I came to the school for nothing today, since Louis suddenly told me he wanted to spend the afternoon with a friend." She'd asked Florence to take him home for lunch, then bring him to and from soccer practice for her. "So it's the perfect opportunity for us to get acquainted!"

The look on Monsieur George's face was priceless. You'd think the man had never been face to face with a determined mother before. He let himself be led by the elbow, though. "I don't really—"

"I have the perfect dish waiting in the oven at home. It was originally a Moroccan recipe. Pie with lamb, ginger, chickpeas, you get the idea. I'm not a big fan of lamb myself, so I've changed it to pork—which means the recipe isn't all that Moroccan anymore. But it's still delicious! And I absolutely insist that you come home and help me eat it, since Louis left me all alone."

"I was going to—"

Christine squeezed his elbow as she peered up at him. "You don't have a wife waiting for you at home, do you?"

"No, but—"

"Then it's settled! You're eating my spicy Moroccan dish and you can tell me all about how you manage to inspire your students. I'm thoroughly impressed!"

Five minutes and endless chatter later, they reached Christine's home. She shoved the teacher ahead of her and had him sit down at the kitchen table.

"Beautiful house you have here, Madame Blanc," he said. "And your garden's gorgeous." He seemed to have accepted his fate for the afternoon.

Christine still locked the front door and hid the key in a drawer.

"Thank you," she said as she pulled her pie from the oven. "It's a lot of work, but the result makes it worth it. Like having kids, I guess."

He pointed to the back of the yard. "Is that a well?"

"Used to be. It was already dry when we bought the house five years ago, and the sellers told us they'd never seen any water down there in ten years. It's very pretty though, with that wooden lid and the little contraption on top."

Christine cut the pie carefully, making six slices, and sliding one piece onto Monsieur George's place and one from the opposite side of the pie onto hers. "I'm thinking of using the well as a compost dump, actually."

Monsieur George hesitated as he squinted at the well. "How would you get the dirt out afterward?"

"Oh." Christine waved a hand. "I wouldn't. Just figured it would be prettier than that heap I have against the fence back there." She pointed to the far corner of the garden, where she'd created a large heap of grass, branches, and leaves over the years. It was the one ugly spot in her garden, which she otherwise absolutely adored since it was walled in by bushes on all sides, making it her own private little haven.

Monsieur George sniffed the plate in front of him. "This smells delicious."

"Why, thank you!" Christine grabbed a bottle of red she'd opened before leaving for school. "Here, have some wine. It's quite strong and goes perfectly with this dish."

"I really shouldn't…"

Christine filled his glass, then filled her own with water. "*Bon appétit!*"

cs

"Ah, you've vacuumed. Excellent." Gérard smiled at his wife and gave her a kiss on the top of her head.

"Yes," Christine replied. "Let me just put the vacuum away and dinner will be ready in five minutes."

Gérard stayed by the couch, his head cocked. "No music today?"

Christine smiled, genuinely this time. "He's out with his friends. Going to the movies, I think."

"Did he finish his homework?"

Rolling her eyes inside the closet as she put the vacuum away, Christine replied, "It's the last week of school, Gérard. There's no homework."

"Right. By the way, I had lunch with Cédric today."

Christine started setting the table. "Léna's dad?"

"Yes." Gérard set out two glasses and the trivet. "Did you know one of the teachers has gone missing?"

Christine filled the mug with water and set it on the table. "Yes. I believe I told you about it. The Automation teacher hasn't been heard from in three weeks."

Gérard shrugged, accepting that he'd forgotten yet another thing she'd told him. "Well, apparently, the police are interviewing the kids and the parents, and since I had an hour to kill this afternoon, I called them."

"How did that go?" Christine set the casserole on the trivet and took her seat.

"They asked if we'd seen anything on the Wednesday he'd gone missing. Also where we'd been. Hah! As if one of the parents would take off with the Automation teacher!"

"Quite."

"Anyway, I told them I'd been at work and that you'd been busy all day. I remember it quite clearly. You'd been really busy that Wednesday. Vacuuming, laundry, gardening. That's the day you turned the well into a compost!"

Christine filled her husband's plate, then her own. "Was it? I can hardly tell one Wednesday from the next."

"Oh, yes. I remember. You'd had so much to do, it wasn't even all done when I got home. Vacuum out, clothes on the bed, gardening tools by the door." He gave Christine a big, bright smile. "I don't know how you do it all."

Christine smiled back at her husband. "You'd be surprised what a mother can do once she sets her mind to it."

THANK YOU

THANK YOU FOR reading *Out of Sight*. I hope you enjoyed it!

The spark of inspiration that started this story is that, like Christine, I sometimes feel like I have to leave out proof of what I've done around the house for it to be acknowledged. Luckily, the rest of the story is pure fiction. I sure had fun writing it, though!

If you liked the story, you might want to check out some of my other books mentioned on the next page. It's mostly Mysteries, but a few Science Fiction short stories will pop up, too.

And don't forget that the first book of my *Tolosa Mystery* series, *The Red Brick Haze*, is available for free on my website.

R.W. Wallace
www.rwwallace.com

Also by R.W. Wallace

Mystery

The Tolosa Mystery Series
The Red Brick Haze (free)
The Red Brick Cellars
The Red Brick Basilica

Ghost Detective Shorts (coming soon)
Just Desserts
Lost Friends
Family Bonds
Till Death
Family History
Common Ground
Heritage
Eternal Bond
New Beginnings

Short Stories
Cold Blue Eternity
Hidden Horrors
Critters
Gertrude and the Trojan Horse
First Impressions
Let Them Eat Cake
Out of Sight
Two's Company
Like Mother Like Daughter

Fantasy (short stories)
Unexpected Consequences
Morbier Impossible
A Second Chance

Science Fiction (short stories)
The Vanguard

Lollapalooza Shorts
Quarantine
Common Enemies
Coiled Danger
Mars Meeting

Adventure (short stories)
Size Matters

www.ingramcontent.com/pod-product-compliance
Lightning Source LLC
LaVergne TN
LVHW041718060526
838201LV00043B/804